Josefina's

Short Story
Collection

BELONGS TO

_____

_____

_____

DATE

Read all of the novels about Josefina:

Meet Josefina
Josefina Learns a Lesson
Josefina's Surprise
Happy Birthday, Josefina!
Josefina Saves the Day
Changes for Josefina
Secrets in the Hills: A Josefina Mystery

·JOSEFINA·

The adventures of *Josefina Montoya* continue in this keepsake collection of short stories. Josefina's growing up under the peaceful blue skies of New Mexico. The traditions of her Mamá, who recently died, are a comfort to shy Josefina. Yet she can't help but be excited about the bold new ideas Tía Dolores brings with her from Mexico City. In her own quiet way, Josefina learns to open her heart to change while still holding on to all that is precious from her past.

Discover more about Josefina's world in these heartwarming stories of deep faith and shining hope.

Josefina's
SHORT STORY
COLLECTION

By VALERIE TRIPP

ILLUSTRATIONS BY JEAN-PAUL TIBBLES

VIGNETTES BY SUSAN McALILEY,

PHILIP HOOD, AND RENÉE GRAEF

⭐ American Girl™

Published by Pleasant Company Publications
Copyright © 2006 by American Girl, LLC

Questions or comments? Call 1-800-845-0005,
visit our Web site at **americangirl.com**, or write to Customer Service,
American Girl, 8400 Fairway Place, Middleton, WI 53562-0497.

Printed in China
06 07 08 09 10 11 LEO 12 11 10 9 8 7 6 5 4 3 2 1

American Girl™ and its associated logos,
Josefina®, and Josefina Montoya® are trademarks of American Girl, LLC.

**Cataloging-in-Publication Data
available from the Library of Congress.**

TABLE OF CONTENTS

JOSEFINA'S FAMILY
AND FRIENDS

page 1
JUST JOSEFINA
When her relatives visit, Josefina is torn between her
grandmother's traditions and her aunt's new ways.
Can Josefina please her family and be true to herself?

page 49
THANKS TO JOSEFINA
Josefina and her sisters are hard at work weaving—
and squabbling. Can Josefina weave together her
sisters' talents and make their chores more fun?

page 93
A REWARD FOR JOSEFINA
Josefina longs for praise from Tía Dolores. She
earns it with some help from someone—and
something—unexpected!

page 135

AGAIN, JOSEFINA!

Josefina is about to give up learning
to play the piano when a small inspiration
convinces her to try again.

page 175

JOSEFINA'S SONG

When a sudden storm puts Josefina and Papá in
danger, it's up to Josefina to get them both to safety.

Josefina's Family

Papá
Josefina's father, who guides his family and his rancho with quiet strength

Josefina
A girl whose heart and hopes are as big as the New Mexico sky

Ana
Josefina's oldest sister, who is married and has two little boys

Francisca
Josefina's second oldest sister, who is headstrong and impatient

Clara
Josefina's practical, sensible sister, who is three years older than Josefina

ABUELITO
*Josefina's grandfather,
a trader who lives in
Santa Fe*

ABUELITA
*Josefina's gracious,
dignified grandmother,
who values tradition*

TÍA DOLORES
*Josefina's aunt, who
has lived far away in
Mexico City for ten years*

**ANTONIO
AND JUAN**
Ana's little boys

TERESITA
Tía Dolores's servant,
an excellent weaver

SANTIAGO
The shepherd at
the Montoyas' camp in
the mountains

ANGELITO
Santiago's nine-year-old
grandson

Josefina and her family speak Spanish, so you'll see some Spanish words in this book. If you can't tell what a word means from reading the story or looking at the illustrations, you can turn to the Glossary of Spanish Words on page 214. It will tell you what the word means and how to pronounce it.

Remember that in Spanish, "j" is pronounced like "h." That means Josefina's name is pronounced "ho-seh-FEE-nah."

JUST JOSEFINA

JUST
JOSEFINA

Josefina stood outside the gate to the
house and leaned forward, shading her
eyes. Did she see a cloud of dust on the
horizon? She held her breath and listened.
Surely that low rumble she heard was
the sound of a wagon lumbering
toward the *rancho*. Oh, she hoped
so! All day while doing her chores,
Josefina had been on the lookout,
watching and listening for a wagon.
Josefina bounced on her toes, too excited

to stand still. It was always a treat when her grandparents, Abuelito and Abuelita, came from their home in Santa Fe to visit. And today, *today*, they were bringing Tía Dolores with them. Josefina couldn't wait.

Josefina felt gentle hands on her shoulders. She turned and saw her papá. Papá didn't say anything, but he stood behind Josefina and watched the dust cloud come closer and closer until, at last, the noisy wagon appeared in the middle of it. They saw Abuelito take off his hat and wave it at them.

Josefina bounced again. By now her sisters, Ana, Francisca, and Clara, were lined up next to Papá to greet their guests. Josefina knew her sisters wanted to dash down the road as much as she did, waving their arms and shouting their happy hellos. But they all knew that would not be proper. So they stood, polite and impatient, while the wagon lurched and rattled to the gate and stopped.

"Welcome," said Papá. He held his hand up to help Tía Dolores down from the wagon.

"*Gracias,*" said Tía Dolores. She smiled, and all the sisters beamed. They were so glad to see her! "And thank you for your kind welcome," she added.

"*Sí, sí,* we thank you," said Abuelito as he climbed down from the wagon. "And we thank God for our safe journey."

"Safe it may have been," said

Abuelita, thumping her skirts so that her own private cloud of dust rose up around her. "Comfortable it was not."

"Ah, my dear!" exclaimed Abuelito. "But here we are! And what an important day this is. For the first time, the first time *ever*, our whole family here on earth is gathered in one spot. How blessed we are! How—"

"Yes, dear," Abuelita spoke over him. "Very true. But now I must get inside."

Josefina stepped forward. "May I help you, Abuelita?" she asked.

"Ah, yes. Gracias, dear child," said Abuelita. "I'm so coated with dust, I feel like a floury *tortilla*." As Josefina helped her grandmother out of the wagon,

"Gracias, dear child," said Abuelita.
"I'm so coated with dust, I feel like a floury tortilla."

Abuelita spoke over her shoulder to Abuelito. "Bring my traveling bag," she ordered him.

The sisters exchanged little half-smiles. They were quite used to the way Abuelita bossed everyone, even Abuelito. When she was safely on the ground, Abuelita let go of Josefina and picked up her skirts in both hands. Like a stately queen, she sailed through the gate with Abuelito following after. But Josefina and her sisters stayed behind with Tía Dolores and Papá, who was directing the servants to unload Tía Dolores's huge trunk from the wagon and carry it to the room that was to be hers.

That trunk has traveled a long, long way, Josefina thought. *I wonder what's inside it.*

For ten years, since before Josefina was born, Tía Dolores had lived in Mexico City. Then, at the end of the summer, she had surprised everyone by returning to New Mexico with Abuelito's caravan. Now it was early fall, and after a short visit to Santa Fe, Tía Dolores had come to live on Papá's rancho with Josefina and her sisters. Their mother had died more than a year ago, and the sisters were struggling to manage the household. Tía Dolores had promised to stay as long as they needed her.

Josefina was even more curious about her tall, energetic aunt than she was about the trunk. Tía Dolores was not beautiful, exactly. But there was a liveliness about her and a look of alert intelligence that Josefina liked. Tía Dolores did not act like other women Josefina knew. She walked across the courtyard with long, confident strides and asked Papá questions about the rancho in a very direct and interested way.

After her trunk was put in its place and Papá and the servants had left the room, Tía Dolores turned to the girls. "I've got so many things to show you," she said. "Do you want to help me unpack?"

"Sí," all four sisters said eagerly.

Tía Dolores unfastened the straps
and lifted the lid of her trunk.

"Ohhh," sighed Ana, Francisca, Clara,
and Josefina in one voice. It was as if Tía
Dolores had opened a treasure chest. The
sisters breathed in a luxurious scent as
luscious as roses in sunshine. The trunk
seemed to overflow with colors. Francisca,
always the boldest, stepped closer.

"Go ahead," Tía Dolores encouraged
her, smiling.

Francisca took a beautiful red shawl
out of the trunk. She wrapped it around
her shoulders, then twirled so that the
fringe on the shawl fluttered. Tía Dolores
and all the sisters laughed aloud in
delight. After that, Ana shyly tried a hair

comb, and Clara inspected a lovely little case that held shiny scissors and pins. Josefina saw a sash made of material as orange as the setting sun. She lifted it out of the trunk and was surprised to feel how light it was. The material was satiny to the touch and smooth as water.

"Look at this, Josefina," Tía Dolores

said. She handed Josefina a small book bound in soft leather. Josefina had seen very, very few books in her life and never one bound so prettily as this. "Open it," said Tía Dolores.

Josefina started to. But just then, Papá stuck his head in the door.

"Josefina," he said. "Abuelita is waiting."

"Oh!" exclaimed Josefina. "Sí, Papá." Quickly, she handed the orange sash and the pretty book to Tía Dolores. "I must go, Tía Dolores," she said.

"Certainly," said Tía Dolores.

Josefina hurried as she crossed the courtyard to Abuelita's room. She'd been so distracted by Tía Dolores and her fascinating trunk that she had forgotten her special duty. She was *always* the one who helped Abuelita get settled when she came to visit.

"Ah, here you are!" said Abuelita when Josefina came in. "You're the only one who can soothe my jangled nerves after that long, hot journey. Just you, Josefina. You're patient and quiet, like your dear mamá."

Josefina felt a rush of love for Abuelita. What an honor it was to be singled out from among her sisters to be Abuelita's preferred helper! And how kind Abuelita was to say that Josefina was like Mamá. No praise could please Josefina more. No praise could make her prouder.

Quietly, Josefina poured Abuelita a
drink of cold, refreshing lemon water.
Then she brought Abuelita a bowl
of cool water that had mint
leaves floating in it. She
gave Abuelita a clean linen
hand cloth and a bar of lavender soap.
While Abuelita washed off the dust of
the road, Josefina unpacked her traveling
bag for her. Carefully, Josefina shook the
wrinkles out of Abuelita's dark, somber
clothes and hung them on pegs. Neatly,
she folded Abuelita's black *rebozo* and
placed it on the *banco*.

"Thank you, dear child," said
Abuelita. "I'll rest now." She sank back
into her chair, put her feet up on a stool,

and closed her eyes.

Josefina knelt on the floor next to Abuelita's chair. As she had done so many times before, she sang softly to ease Abuelita to sleep. She sang the same slow, soft, sweet song she always sang for Abuelita. But suddenly, her song was interrupted. Happy whoops of laughter looped across the courtyard. Josefina stopped singing and listened to her sisters and Tía Dolores laughing together. *What are they all having so much fun about?* she wondered.

Abuelita patted Josefina's hand. "Ignore those noisy hens!" she said.

Josefina tried, but she couldn't ignore the laughter. She couldn't ignore an itchy impatience she felt, either. *I wish Abuelita would hurry up and fall asleep so that I could go join my sisters and Tía Dolores,* Josefina thought. *I wish* . . . She stopped herself. She was shocked at her own thoughts and shivered as if to shake off a terrible suspicion. Maybe she wasn't the patient and quiet child Abuelita thought she was. Maybe she wasn't like Mamá after all.

❅

A few days later, Josefina and her sisters spent a happy afternoon picking apples with Tía Dolores. Neighbors were coming that evening, and the cook needed apples to make *empanaditas* to serve.

"I'm looking forward to seeing everyone tonight," said Tía Dolores as they walked back to the rancho from the orchard with their baskets full.

It was the custom at harvest time for neighbors to help one another. Tonight everyone was gathering at Papá's to help string chile peppers into *ristras*. People told jokes and stories as they worked, and sometimes there was music.

"I hope there'll be dancing," said Francisca. "I'd love to show off that new dance you taught us, Tía Dolores." She held her basket of apples steady on her head with one hand, held her skirt with her other hand, and

16

danced along the road humming the music. It looked like so much fun that soon Ana, Clara, and Josefina were dancing, too. Josefina skipped and twirled and danced ahead of the others, her feet flying all the rest of the way to the gate of the house.

"That was wonderful, Josefina!" said Tía Dolores.

"You do that dance almost as well as I do," said Francisca, who prided herself on being the best dancer in the family. "And you surely do it *faster* than all of the rest of us." Clara and Ana agreed.

Josefina twirled once more, then curtsied. "Gracias," she said. She liked the dance. It was exuberant and a little

17

wild. It made her feel happy and free.

Inside the gate, Abuelita met them. "Look at you!" she said, smiling but sounding a little exasperated. "Your clothes are mussed. Your hands are scratched. You have twigs in your hair."

"We've been picking apples," said Tía Dolores.

"And now your noses are as red as apples," said Abuelita, shaking her head. "I gave up on your ruddy complexion long ago, Dolores. But, girls, how many times have I told you to shade your faces? You'll ruin your skin." Abuelita sighed. "Hurry along now, and tidy yourselves," she ordered, fluttering her hands at the sisters as if she were scattering chickens.

"Our guests will be here soon. Josefina, you come with me."

Obediently, Josefina followed Abuelita into her cool, shadowy room.

"I have something special for you to wear tonight," said Abuelita. She handed Josefina a pretty skirt. It was blue with a shiny black ribbon at the hem.

"Oh, Abuelita!" said Josefina, delighted. "It's beautiful. Gracias."

"Put it on," said Abuelita.

Josefina slipped off the old skirt she'd worn apple picking and carefully stepped into the new one. She had to hold her breath to button the skirt. It fit, but only just. It was very, very tight around her waist.

But Abuelita did not notice. "That skirt belonged to your mamá," she said, her eyes bright. "I want you to have it because you remind me of her so much. You have the same small hands and round cheeks, the same sweet voice, and the same sweet disposition. She was shy and obedient like you." Abuelita smiled. "Not like my adventurous Dolores!"

"Gracias, Abuelita," said Josefina again, straight from her heart. She was grateful for Abuelita's gift and even more thankful for Abuelita's compliments. She hugged her grandmother—but carefully.

She did not want to pop the button off her beautiful blue skirt.

"Are you feeling all right, Josefina?" Tía Dolores asked her that evening. "You are so quiet. And you haven't eaten a bite."

Josefina blushed. "I am very well, thank you, Tía Dolores," she said, even though the truth was that she could hardly breathe. She could not tell Tía Dolores that she wasn't talking or eating because Mamá's skirt was strangling her around the waist! She could not bend or stoop. She had to sit uncomfortably stiff and straight, which made it hard to string the chiles. She had to say no thank you when some of the children invited her to play a running game. And when the grownups began telling jokes and stories, Josefina couldn't let herself laugh too much or it would strain her skirt.

It was hard not to laugh, especially when Abuelito told everyone's favorite story, the one about the time he brought Tía Dolores's piano from Mexico City. Of course, Josefina and everyone else had heard many times how thieves attacked the caravan but were frightened away by the thunderous sound of the piano falling off a wagon. But Abuelito made the story funnier every time he told it. Besides, everyone was very interested in Tía Dolores's piano. Most of the guests had never seen or heard a piano in their lives.

"Will you play your piano for us?" Papá asked Tía Dolores after Abuelito had finished his story.

"I'd be pleased to," Tía Dolores said. She rose and led the way to the *gran sala*.

At first, everyone stood politely and listened to the music. But then Tía Dolores began to play a dance tune that was so lively, no one could resist it. Couples began dancing. Those too old to dance sat and clapped and nodded their heads in time to the music. Those too young to dance, like Clara and Josefina, tapped their feet and jigged in place. Soon, the whole room was full of movement. The music swooped and swirled around them, encircling them with its energy. One dance led to another, and another.

Josefina moved next to the piano so that she could watch Tía Dolores's fingers fly over the keys. Suddenly, Tía Dolores began to play the music that went with the new dance she'd taught Josefina and her sisters.

"Josefina," said Tía Dolores over the music. "Show everyone the new dance I taught you. You dance it so well."

Before Josefina could answer, Abuelita spoke up from her seat near

the piano. "Gracious, Dolores!" Abuelita
exclaimed. "You've brought new notions
from Mexico City as well as new dances.
It is not proper for Josefina to dance in
front of company. She is too young."

"But, Mamá," said Tía Dolores, "the
guests are all old friends and neighbors."

"Nevertheless!" said Abuelita sternly.
"Josefina is not allowed to dance. She
obeys the rules even if you don't. In any
case, little Josefina is far too shy." Abuelita
turned to Josefina and said in a voice
that sounded confident of being obeyed,
"You wouldn't dream of dancing, would
you, pet?"

But dreaming seemed to be just what
Josefina was doing. Because much to her

own surprise, she found herself stepping out onto the floor. As if the music had enchanted her, she began to dance. Josefina's feet hardly touched the ground, she skipped and spun and danced so fast. How wonderful it felt! Josefina listened to the wild, exuberant music and let it carry her without thinking. People clapped for her and stamped their feet so that the floor shook. Soon they joined the dance, too, and Josefina was surrounded by swirling skirts and dancing feet.

Faster and faster Josefina danced until—*pop!* The button on Mamá's skirt shot off. No one else noticed, but Josefina stopped dancing. She clutched her skirt

Josefina's feet hardly touched the ground, she skipped and spun and danced so fast. How wonderful it felt!

to her waist and watched the button spin across the floor and skitter like a bug past the dancers' shoes until it stopped dead, right at Abuelita's feet. With a cold and disapproving frown, Abuelita picked up the button and put it in her pocket.

Josefina's heart thudded as she realized what she had done. She had disobeyed and disappointed Abuelita. Now Abuelita would never feel the same way about her again.

When the dance ended, the evening did, too. Reminding one another that tomorrow was a working day, the guests said good-bye and thank you to Papá, Abuelita, Abuelito, and Tía Dolores. They strolled home under the starry sky,

still humming or whistling the music
that Tía Dolores had played. When the
last guest was gone and the last note had
faded away, Josefina followed Abuelita
to her room to sing her to sleep as she
always did.

But Abuelita dismissed her. "I don't
need you tonight, Josefina," she said
coolly. She closed her door, leaving
Josefina alone.

Josefina crossed the courtyard to
the room she shared with her sisters.
Sadly, she took off the beautiful blue
skirt, folded it carefully, and put it away.

Josefina went to bed, but her heart
was so heavy that she couldn't sleep.
All night she lay awake thinking. By

morning she had decided what she must do. At dawn, she rose quietly and dressed in her work clothes. She picked up the blue skirt and held it close to her chest. Silently, she tiptoed across the courtyard to Abuelita's room. She gave the skirt one last hug, then slowly bent down to put it outside Abuelita's door.

Suddenly, the door opened.

Josefina looked up. Abuelita was standing in the doorway of her room. She seemed small and shadowy in the early morning light.

"I have been waiting for you, Josefina," said Abuelita. "Come in."

Abuelita lit a candle. Then she sat tiredly in her chair and motioned for

Josefina to sit on the floor beside her.
Josefina knew she must not speak first.
She waited anxiously for what Abuelita
was going to say.

"Dear child," Abuelita began. Then
she stopped.

Josefina burst out, "Oh, Abuelita.
I'm sorry. I know I disappointed you

31

when I danced. But Tía Dolores's music made me feel so wonderful, I *had* to dance. I know Mamá never would have done such a thing." Josefina sighed. "I've always been so honored when you've said that I'm like Mamá. But I've learned something about myself. In some ways I am like Mamá, but in some ways I am not." Josefina put the blue skirt on Abuelita's lap. "This is a beautiful skirt, Abuelita," she said. "But it doesn't really fit me. Do you want it back?"

Abuelita stroked the skirt. "I've learned something, too," she said. "I miss your Mamá so much that I look every-where for reminders of her." Abuelita smiled at Josefina, but it was a sad smile.

"I saw many reminders in you, and they comforted me. But that wasn't fair of me. You're not like anyone else, nor should you be. You're yourself, and that's perfect. I love you because you are you."

Josefina rose up on her knees and hugged Abuelita around the waist.

"And as for your blue skirt," said Abuelita, sounding more like her usual bossy self, "you must sew this back on immediately." She pulled the button out of her pocket. "But put it in a different place so that the waistband is looser." She raised her eyebrows as she said, "And you had better sew it on good and tight, in case you decide to dance again."

"Sí," said Josefina happily.

Abuelita was happy, too. "The skirt belongs to you now," she said. "You must fix it so that it fits you and no one else—just you, just Josefina."

LOOKING BACK

WOMEN'S RIGHTS
IN 1824

Josefina came from a long line of strong, spirited women. Like Abuelita, Tía Dolores, and Ana, New Mexican women in the early 1800s had many responsibilities. They ran large house-holds and worked with their husbands on ranchos, while also raising and educating their children. These women

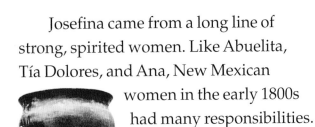

found strength in their faith and family relationships, just as American women of the time did. But New Mexican women had rights and freedoms that American women would not have for many years.

When an American woman in 1824 got married, she took her husband's last name and lost any legal rights of her own. A married woman could not buy or sell property, and her husband took control of any property that was hers before the marriage. She

Land was the most common property that women—both American and New Mexican—brought into a marriage.

could not sign legal documents or appear in courts of law. And although she might work outside the home, any wages she earned were controlled by her husband.

New Mexican women, in contrast, had rights that were deeply rooted in Spanish tradition. They kept their maiden names after marriage. They also kept any property that was theirs before marriage,

A New Mexican wedding in the late 1800s

such as money or jewelry passed down to them by their mothers. Whatever a woman owned, she could make decisions about without consulting her husband. She could sell property or pass it down to her own daughter by drawing up a *will,* a document that says what should happen to a person's possessions when she dies.

Under Mexican law, women could have wills created in their own names. The property described in the will could

Wills included long lists of possessions.

be anything from land and herds of
animals to the clothes and household
goods the woman owned at the time
of her death. One will written in 1830
included a silk jacket,
a fringed shawl, and
"three petticoats of
coarse cotton—used."
Mexican law also
gave women the right to protect
their possessions. They could *sue*,
or take to court, anyone who
threatened their property. Some
women sued their own husbands!
Doña Gregoria Quintana took her husband
to court when he sold her grain mill without her consent. The court ordered that

Many women owned silk shawls called **mantóns** *(mahn-TOHNS).*

the new owner of the mill grind a portion of grain for Doña Gregoria each year until her death. Another woman took her husband to court for gambling away her burro. The court ordered that the burro be returned to the wife and fined the husband two pesos for gambling.

New Mexican women in 1824 were free to work outside the home and to keep their earnings. Some, like Doña Gregoria, even owned their own businesses. One of the most successful of

A sturdy burro was valuable property.

these women was Gertrudis Barceló, known as Doña Tules (TOO-lehs). She owned a gambling house in Santa Fe—an unusual business for women of the time. Doña Tules was a skilled card dealer and a smart businesswoman. Her gambling house was popular among Mexican and American soldiers, and Doña Tules became a trusted advisor to both. She also became quite wealthy. When the U.S. Army needed money, it turned to Doña Tules for help!

Many people respected Doña Tules's independence and spirit, but American traders were shocked to see women in gambling halls, smoking and playing cards with men. Americans were also surprised by the clothing worn by New Mexican

Doña Tules, the woman who dared to do men's work

43

women: loose cotton blouses and skirts that revealed their ankles. This clothing was practical in the warm Southwest, but it was very different from the corsets and hoopskirts worn by American women at the time.

As traders brought American goods and ideas south, the free-flowing clothing of New Mexican women gave way to more confining American styles. When New Mexican women became American citizens in 1848, they lost other freedoms, too. Their legal rights didn't hold up in American courts, and women lost some of their independence. But they never lost their spirit. The courage and determination shown by these early New Mexican women are still alive in Hispanic women of today.

This young doctor follows in the footsteps of her Hispanic ancestors, many of whom worked as midwives and healers.

THANKS TO
JOSEFINA

THANKS TO
JOSEFINA

On a bright, blue-sky day in late
October, Josefina Montoya and her
sisters were working in the weaving
room. Ana, the eldest, was weaving at
one of the large looms. She hummed as
she worked, and the peaceful *thump,
thump* of the foot pedals made a rhythm
as gentle as breathing. Francisca was
spinning wool into yarn, and Clara was
carding wool to get the tangles out.
Josefina was half-sitting, half-kneeling in

front of a smaller hanging
loom. Slowly and carefully,
she threaded a strand of
yarn in and out, in and out,
in front of and then behind
the long lengths of yarn that hung taut
between bars at the ceiling and the floor.

"Very good, girls!" said Tía Dolores.
The sisters looked up to see their aunt
watching them from the doorway. "I am
so pleased to find you hard at work.
Bless you!"

"*Gracias*, Tía Dolores," said the
sisters. They smiled at their aunt. Josefina
smiled at Teresita, too, who was standing
behind Tía Dolores. Teresita was Tía
Dolores's servant. She was a wise and

kind Navajo woman who had taught
Josefina how to weave.

"I have good news," Tía Dolores said
cheerfully. "Teresita and I have counted
the sacks of wool in the storeroom, and
there's plenty. Teresita says we should be
able to make a good number of blankets."
A week ago, a terrible flash flood had
killed most of the family's sheep. The
rancho could not survive without sheep to
provide both meat and wool for weaving
and trading. The family was pinning its
hopes on Tía Dolores's idea of using wool
they had in the storeroom
to weave blankets, which
they'd sell or trade to
buy sheep to start a new

51

herd. "The *americanos* come to Santa Fe to trade in the summer," said Tía Dolores, "so that's when we must have our blankets finished."

"That's good news, too," said Francisca. "That means we have plenty of time as well as plenty of wool. Summer's far away."

Tía Dolores was still smiling, but she shook her head. "I am afraid the time will fly by," she said. "We won't have enough blankets unless we all weave as much as we can, as fast as we can."

"Forgive me, Tía Dolores," said Clara. She sounded anxious. "I'm afraid if I weave quickly, I'll make mistakes."

Tía Dolores spoke earnestly. "You'll

do fine, Clara, if you try," she said. "Look at Josefina. She didn't know how to weave at all. But she tried very hard and she learned from Teresita so that now she can help weave, too. And remember, it was Josefina's enthusiasm that encouraged your Papá to agree to our weaving business in the first place. The fact that we're doing it at all is thanks to Josefina."

Josefina cast her eyes down. She blushed at Tía Dolores's praise.

"I have great faith in all of you girls," said Tía Dolores. "You'll work as hard *every* week as you have this first week to make our weaving business a success, won't you?"

"We will, Tía Dolores," promised

Josefina cast her eyes down. She blushed at Tía Dolores's praise.

Ana, Francisca, and Clara.

Josefina promised, too. As usual,
Tía Dolores made everything seem possible. She was so full of energy that some
of it seemed to spill over and splash out
onto everyone around her. But secretly,
Josefina was a little worried. Weaving
was difficult for her. Teresita had taught
her well, and yet she still made so many
mistakes that Teresita often had to tell her
to take out a row and do it over again.
Josefina wondered how much help she
could truly be. Then she squared her
shoulders and pushed her worries away.
With all her heart, she was determined to
keep her promise to Tía Dolores. She was
sure her sisters meant their promises, too.

And they did. All four sisters wove conscientiously and without complaining—for the next few days, anyway.

Then one gray day, not quite two weeks after the flood, Josefina, Clara, and Francisca were in the weaving room before Ana, Teresita, or Tía Dolores had arrived. Josefina and Francisca were picking burrs out of clumps of wool, and Clara was trying to spin wool into yarn. Clara's hands were not quick. Again and again, the spindle bounced and skittered away from her.

"Oh!" Clara wailed. "I hate spinning. I don't like doing things fast. The spindle spins so fast that it makes me dizzy. I feel like a spinning top."

"I feel like a shepherd," Francisca groused, "completely surrounded by wool. Soon I'll *look* like a shepherd, too, because even with all this weaving we're doing, we're not making anything pretty for ourselves to wear."

Josefina decided to try to cheer her sisters. She turned to Francisca and made a comically long face. In a low, sad voice, she sang an old song they all knew:

The life of the shepherd
is the saddest of all,
keeping up with the sheep,
only dressing up on Sundays . . .

Clara laughed. Francisca did, too, but her voice had a sting in it as she said,

"At least I'm not a sheep, Josefina, like you are." Francisca plunked her clump of wool on top of Josefina's head. "You're a baby sheep so eager to please that you follow wherever the shepherd—or in this case, shepherdess—leads."

"Little Josefina," teased Clara, "a little sheep. *Baa, baa, baa.*"

Josefina pretended to smile at her sisters' teasing. When she tried to brush the wool off her head, burrs caught in her hair. She had to pull at the wool, which hurt so badly that it made her eyes water. Her feelings were hurt, too. She was used to Francisca's sharp tongue, but it wasn't like Clara to join Francisca against her. And it wasn't fair. Did her sisters think

she liked sitting there hour after hour
weaving? Did they think she liked undo-
ing her mistakes, no matter how kindly
Teresita asked her to? Well, she did *not*.

Cheerful sunshine slanted through
the open door of the weaving room and

made a bright, inviting path across the floor. Josefina swallowed a sigh. How she wished she could jump up and run outside along that sunny path! But she knew she must not stop weaving, even though she'd been at it so long this morning that her legs, folded beneath her, had fallen asleep. Her arms were so tired that they seemed to want to go to sleep, too.

The weaving business was in its third week now, and things were not going well. Ana's baby son was ill, so Ana had not been able to weave for the past several

days. Tía Dolores and Teresita were so busy washing and dyeing wool that they were seldom in the weaving room, either. All this

morning, Josefina and Clara had had only
each other for company. They both looked
up from their looms when Francisca finally
sashayed into the room.

"Well, well," said Clara. "Here you
are at last."

Francisca yawned extravagantly in
answer. She sat at her loom and began
to weave quickly, carelessly, and noisily.

"You'll make mistakes if you weave
so fast," Clara warned.

Francisca ignored her. If anything,
she began to weave faster.

Clara was annoyed. She looked away
from Francisca and her eyes fell on
Josefina's loom. She stopped weaving
and came over to study Josefina's work.

"You made a mistake, Josefina," she said, pointing. "Look. All of the rows you've done since your mistake will have to be taken out."

Josefina saw that Clara was right. Her heart sank. Two days' worth of weaving would have to be undone and then redone. "I hate having to fix my mistakes," she moaned.

"I'll do it," said Clara eagerly.

"No!" said Josefina. She was angry at herself and angry at Clara because Clara seemed just the tiniest bit pleased to have given her such bad news. Then Josefina saw something that made her angry at Francisca, too. "Francisca, what are you doing?" Josefina asked. "That's my red wool you're using. Stop!"

Francisca didn't stop. She shrugged. "Use my wool if you're in such a hurry," she said.

"But your red wool is knotty," said Josefina. "You dyed it red while it still had burrs in it."

"No one will notice a few burrs in your bumpy mess of a blanket," Francisca said coolly. "At least I—" But just then, Josefina snatched the red wool away from her. "Give it back," Francisca demanded. "Don't be so stingy. You're not using it."

"Not yet," replied Josefina, "but—"

"Not any time soon," Clara cut in. "You are the slowest weaver in the world, Josefina, even on that little loom."

"You're not very fast, either," said Josefina hotly.

"I'm slow but I'm steady," said Clara. "I don't make mistakes the way you and Francisca do."

"Your blankets are dull," Francisca said to Clara.

"Dull?" Clara repeated.

"*Sí*," Francisca said. "Duller than the wool that's still on the sheep! I'm the only one who truly knows how to put the colors together." This was true. Josefina and Clara could not deny that Francisca's blankets were the most beautiful. Francisca added, "And I'm the fastest weaver, too."

64

"Because you're the most careless," Josefina said.

"When you bother to weave at all," said Clara, "which is hardly ever."

"You expect us to card your wool for you," said Josefina.

"I hate to card wool," said Francisca. "It's too slow."

"Well, I hate to spin wool," said Clara. "It's too fast."

"And I hate taking out mistakes and starting over," said Josefina.

At that, both Clara and Francisca whirled to face Josefina. "You should have thought of that before you got us into the weaving business," said Clara.

"Yes," said Francisca. "It's all your

fault. As Tía Dolores said, we're in this business thanks to *you*, Josefina!"

Josefina could stand no more. She jumped to her feet and stormed out, leaving her loom in a knotted, tangled mess. Her feelings were knotted and tangled, too, and her cheeks felt hot. She was sure that they were as red as the wool she had jammed into her pocket so that Francisca couldn't use it.

Josefina yanked the door to the weaving room shut behind her and ran to the little flower garden her mother had planted in a corner of the courtyard. She knelt down by the flowers and tried to calm herself. The flowers had been battered by the storm that had caused the flood. They leaned every which way, and some lay flat in the dirt. Josefina tried to straighten them and help them stand up, but they flopped down, defeated and disheartened, as soon as she took her hand away. Josefina swiped away a tear. She felt defeated and disheartened, too. She had never had such a terrible fight with her sisters before.

"Ah, Josefina!" said Teresita, coming toward her. "Here you are. I couldn't find you in the weaving room. I need your help. I'm going up into the hills to gather plants to make dyes. Your Tía Dolores says you know all the best places to look for plants. Will you come with me?"

Josefina could only nod.

"Good, then," said Teresita, handing Josefina a collecting basket like the one she carried. If she noticed Josefina's red, tear-streaked cheeks, she was too polite and kind to say anything about them.

As Teresita and Josefina climbed up the hill behind the orchard, a brisk, playful wind cooled Josefina's cheeks. Teresita

walked quickly. Josefina, stretching her
legs to keep up, felt the tight knot of
anger inside her chest stretch and loosen,
too. It was impossible to be downhearted
under such a blue, blue sky decorated
with high white clouds. It felt wonderful
to Josefina to be outside, moving freely.

It felt wonderful to be helpful, too.
Josefina knew where to find all the plants
Teresita needed.

"Have you seen *cañaigre* growing on
this hillside?" Teresita asked.

"Sí!" said Josefina. "Follow me!" She
led Teresita to a sunny spot where cañaigre plants grew thick.

"We'll slice and dry these cañaigre
roots to make gold and orange dyes,"

Teresita told Josefina as they put some roots in their baskets.

Josefina found *capulín* bushes for Teresita and helped her pick the berries, which Teresita said made dark pink dye. When Teresita asked for rabbit brush, Josefina led her to a hillside covered with it. "Rabbit brush blossoms make a lovely yellow dye," said Teresita.

"And Mamá told me the stems make green dye," Josefina said.

"That's right," said Teresita.

"I know where there are walnut trees, too," said Josefina eagerly. "Mamá taught me that walnut hulls make good dark brown and black dyes."

Teresita smiled. "I can see that I chose a very good helper," she said. "Lead the way, Josefina."

After they collected the walnuts, Josefina and Teresita walked back to the rancho. "I have such a funny collection of things in my basket," Josefina said, swinging her basket beside her. "Stems, roots, blossoms, berries, and nuts."

"Each one is important and necessary," said Teresita, "because each one makes a different color dye."

"These roots and berries are sort of like people," Josefina said. "Different ones are good at different things."

"Sí," agreed Teresita. "And we need the different abilities that people have,

*"These roots and berries are sort of like people," Josefina said.
"Different ones are good at different things."*

just as we need all the different colors, to make our blankets beautiful."

Josefina was quiet, thinking about what Teresita had said. It reminded her of her sisters. Each sister was good at what she *liked* to do and not so good at what she did *not* like to do. Clara didn't mind carding, but she hated to spin because it was too fast. Francisca hated to card because it was too slow, but she was good at spinning and choosing colors. Josefina hated to undo her weaving mistakes, but Clara liked taking out rows. Maybe they could help one another. Instead of each sister doing all the steps in weaving, maybe each could do only the step she liked best.

Josefina put her free hand in her pocket and pulled out her red wool. *Would her idea work?* she wondered. She grinned to herself. One thing was for sure—it could not make things worse. *It's worth a try*, she decided.

❋

Josefina was in front of her loom, carding wool, when Clara and Francisca came into the weaving room the next morning.

"What's this?" asked Francisca. She picked up a thick skein of beautiful, per-fect red wool from the stool at her loom.

"Oh, I prepared that for you," said Josefina.

Francisca raised her eyebrows. "Gracias," she said. "But why?"

"Well," said Josefina, "in return, I'd like you to help Clara choose colors for her blanket. Will you?"

"Sí," said Francisca. "I'd like to, but . . ." She looked at Clara uncertainly.

Clara smiled. "I could use your help," she admitted.

"And Clara," said Josefina, "when you have time, could you help me?" She nodded at the tangled mess on her loom. "Will you take out these rows and help me fix the mistake I made?"

"I'd be glad to," said Clara. "That's work I like to do."

Francisca put her hands on her hips.

"What's going on here, Josefina?" she asked.

Josefina shrugged and grinned. "I just thought we could help one another," she said simply. "We'll all keep on weaving, of course, but we can share the other work. Each one of us can do the parts we like to do."

Francisca and Clara looked at each other and burst out laughing. "That's a wonderful idea, Josefina," Francisca said. "I'm good at doing things I like to do!"

"We all are," said Clara.

Josefina smiled. "I have another idea, too," she said. "Would you like to go on a picnic tomorrow? We can go up into the hills, and I will show you the plants that make the dyes. Teresita taught me some new ones."

"That would be fun!" said Francisca.

"Having fun is something we are all very good at, isn't it?" joked Josefina.

Her sisters certainly agreed. And, as the days went on, they also agreed that Josefina's idea about helping one another made weaving much more pleasant. The weaving business went smoothly— thanks to Josefina.

LOOKING BACK

BLANKETS IN 1824

Blankets woven by New Mexicans in Josefina's time were as beautiful as the land they came from. They were made of the soft wool of the *churro* sheep that were raised on the ranchos. The wool was colored with rich yellow, gold, and dark brown dyes made from the plants and trees that grew nearby. And the blankets were brightened with bits of red wool and bands of indigo wool as blue as the New Mexican sky.

A New Mexican blanket woven in the mid-1800s

Each beautiful blanket
required many hours of
hard work. After men
sheared the sheep, women
and girls washed the wool
and removed any burrs
or twigs. Then they
used brushes to *card*, or
untangle, the wool. Next,
they prepared dyes using
roots, berries, blossoms, and
nuts they had gathered.

Carding brushes had stiff bristles for untangling wool.

New Mexicans also used
dyes imported from farther
south in Mexico, such as indigo and
cochineal. *Indigo* was a deep blue dye
made from plants, which could be used

81

These dried insects were ground into powder to make cochineal.

alone or mixed with yellow dye to create green. *Cochineal* was a crimson red dye made from tiny insects. Each pound of cochineal required 70,000 insects, so the dye was very expensive. No wonder Josefina guarded her red wool closely!

Weavers spun the dyed wool into yarn and used it to create colorful patterns on their blankets. They wove stripes of blue, brown, yellow, and white wool, and perhaps a stripe or two of the cherished red wool. Some weavers added diamond, leaf, or zigzag designs borrowed from Saltillo *sarapes*, finely woven ponchos made in Saltillo and other towns in northern Mexico.

Navajo Indians wove blankets with designs similar to those woven into their baskets. They wove rows of triangles or the "Spider Woman's Cross," named after the mythical woman who taught the Navajo how to weave. Blankets woven by Indian servants in

A basket and dress showing the Spider Woman's Cross

New Mexican households came to be known as "servant blankets." They often showed a combination of Navajo and New Mexican designs.

One such blanket was woven by a Navajo servant named Rosario. Rosario had been taken captive by Spanish settlers and brought to live with a priest named Padre Martínez. Rosario missed her people, but the padre was kind to her, and she eventually

made a new life with him. When, years later, he offered Rosario her freedom, she chose to stay with him. To thank him for his kindness, she wove him a sarape. She thought,

I'll make it a bit Navajo and the rest Spanish, for I am both now. I'll use white for the pureness, nobleness and sincerity of the padre, and I'll use black for the sorrow I . . . went through many years ago. And I'll put in red for the courage we all have to have.

Rosario wove on a Navajo loom much like Teresita's.

Both Indians and New Mexicans wove blankets as thank-you gifts for personal favors. Blankets were also given to new brides as wedding gifts from the groom's family. These blankets were made of silky white wool and usually had a single brown stripe at the center. Small bits of colored yarn were added later to give new life to old blankets.

Most blankets, though, were made for use in the weaver's own household or for trade. New Mexicans wove thick wool sarapes to wear in the winter or to use as sleeping blankets at night. Weavers

The dashes of red and blue wool were added long after this wedding blanket was woven.

This Mexican man wears a colorful sarape.

made other blankets to use as rugs, saddle blankets, wall coverings, and padding on *bancos*, or benches.

Blankets were also woven to trade in Mexico City for necessities like iron tools and dry goods and for luxuries like chocolate and china. New Mexicans traded blankets to Indians in exchange for pottery, baskets, and buffalo hides. And when the Santa Fe Trail opened in 1821, New Mexicans began trading with Americans as well.

Trade with Americans would change weaving in many ways. Americans brought cotton cloth and ready-made clothing, which meant New Mexicans began weaving less clothing and more blankets for trade. In the 1860s, Americans introduced *aniline* or artificial dyes, and in the 1870s, machine-spun yarns. These dyes and yarns made weaving easier,

American traders also brought shoes, glass bottles, toys, mirrors, and tools.

but aniline dyes faded over time, so blankets didn't retain their beauty.

Today, some New Mexicans continue to weave blankets with real wool and natural dyes. In Chimayó, New Mexico, there are families who have been in business since the early 1700s. The traditional methods take time, but the finished blankets provide a valuable—and colorful—link to New Mexico's past.

A REWARD FOR
JOSEFINA

A Reward for Josefina

Josefina walked quickly and skipped
every few steps to match Tía Dolores's
long strides. It was just before dawn on a
cold, clear day. Josefina and Tía Dolores
were walking up into the foothills of the
mountains to gather *piñón* nuts. Papá
was ahead of them, and Josefina
could hear her sisters behind her,
huffing and puffing as the path
grew steeper.

Josefina liked the energetic way

Tía Dolores walked. In fact, she liked everything about her young aunt—from her wholehearted way of laughing to her strong, square hands to the way Tía Dolores listened, *really* listened, when Josefina spoke. Tía Dolores had recently come to live on Papá's *rancho*. Josefina and her sisters wanted Tía Dolores to be happy there, and so each sister tried hard in her own way to please her.

"Look," said Josefina, pointing. "The sun's coming up over the mountain."

"Ah!" said Tía Dolores. She smiled, first at the sun and then at Josefina. "God has given us a fine day."

"*Sí*," said Clara, Josefina's next oldest sister. "A fine day for our hard work."

"Look," said Josefina, pointing. "The sun's coming up over the mountain."

"Oh, Clara," laughed Josefina. "Gathering piñón nuts isn't *work*. It's fun."

But Clara wanted Tía Dolores to know how practical she was. "It's important that we gather a good harvest of piñón nuts," she said seriously. "Papá trades them for things we need. They're valuable."

"They're delicious!" said Francisca, Josefina's second oldest sister, who never worried about being practical. Francisca ran ahead, then turned around and walked backward so that she was facing Tía Dolores. "On winter evenings," she said, "we sit by the fire and roast the nuts and crack them and eat them, one after another! Oh, it makes me hungry just to *think* of it!"

"Don't get hungry yet," warned Ana. "Lunchtime is hours away." Ana was the oldest sister. She had helped Carmen, the cook, pack a lunch for everyone to enjoy at noon. It was carefully wrapped in a sack that was tied to the mule Carmen's husband Miguel was leading. Ana's little boy Juan was on the mule, too. Juan was only three, and his legs were so short they stuck straight out on either side of the mule's back. Ana carried her baby, Antonio, on her hip. He was only one year old and too little to ride the mule.

Tía Dolores lifted Antonio out of

Ana's arms. "Let me carry this stout fellow," she said.

"*Gracias*," said Ana. She and Tía Dolores exchanged a smile.

When Josefina saw that smile she felt a terrible pang of jealousy. She knew she shouldn't envy Ana the special affection and respect that Tía Dolores had for her. After all, Tía Dolores and Ana were close in age. It made sense that they were more like friends than aunt and niece. And sweet, gentle Ana deserved Tía Dolores's respect. Hadn't she taken over the responsibility of running the household since Mamá's death over a year ago? But Josefina couldn't help envying Ana. Tía Dolores was always kind and loving to

Josefina, of course. But with all her heart, Josefina wanted Tía Dolores to smile at her the way she smiled at Ana—with pride. She longed for Tía Dolores to think of her as someone special.

Francisca had moved ahead of the rest of them along the path. She called back now, "Hurry up! Papá's waiting for us." The sun caught the frost on the pine trees and made it sparkle. Francisca had thrown back her *rebozo*, and Josefina could see sparkles in her hair, too, where frost had fallen on it. Josefina sighed. Francisca was just naturally special. She could always make Tía Dolores laugh because she was so quick and lively. And Clara had already

rebozo

won Tía Dolores's praise for being
careful with her sewing and weaving.

*Maybe today will be my chance to
impress Tía Dolores*, thought Josefina.
*Maybe I could save her from twisting her
ankle, or falling off a cliff, or being eaten by a
mountain lion!* Then Josefina laughed at
herself. She knew perfectly well that Tía
Dolores was the most surefooted of them
all. And if a mountain lion should
happen to bump into Tía Dolores,
Josefina could easily picture her aunt
shooing it away all on her own.

Papá was waiting for them in a
clearing surrounded by scrub oaks,

cottonwoods, and a few piñon trees. "This is a good place to build our fire," he said. "We'll spread out from here to gather nuts from the trees on the hillside, then we'll meet back here for lunch at noon." His eyes twinkled as he spoke to the sisters and Tía Dolores. "You'll have to earn your lunch today. It will be your reward for a sack full of piñon nuts. And this year, I'm offering a special reward to the one who gathers the most nuts. We'll see whose sack is biggest at noontime."

All the sisters smiled. Josefina was so happy she wanted to cheer out loud. At last! Here was her chance to shine! She was determined that no one would collect more piñon nuts than she would.

Papá's reward—and Tía Dolores's admiration—would be hers.

Josefina picked up an empty sack. Her hopes were high, and she was eager to begin gathering. But Papá's next words sent her hopes crashing down. "Josefina, my little one," he said. "You stay here and help Carmen and Miguel. Keep the fire going, and keep an eye on Antonio and Juan."

"But *I* want to go, too!" wailed Juan. "I want to collect nuts and win the reward!" Josefina was glad. Juan had said aloud exactly what she was thinking!

Papá knelt next to Juan. "You and Josefina have a different job to do," he

said. "We'll be hungry when we return
from gathering nuts. We'll be very disappointed if animals have stolen our
lunch away! You must guard it for us."
Papá smiled up at Josefina, saying,
"That's a very important job, isn't it,
Josefina?"

"Sí, Papá," said Josefina. Papá's

smile was warm, and Josefina tried hard
to return it as she handed her sack back
to him. But she was brokenhearted!
*I've just lost my best chance to impress
Tía Dolores*, she thought. *How can I collect
any nuts left behind here with the lunch and
the babies?*

Sadly, Josefina watched Papá and
Tía Dolores and her sisters walk away.
Their laughter and happy chatter faded
as they disappeared among the trees,
and soon it was quiet in the clearing.
Carmen spread a blanket on the ground,
and Juan and Antonio fell asleep on it.

Josefina helped Miguel start a fire,
and then Carmen asked her to stir a pot
of chile stew as it simmered. Josefina

was grumpy. *I might just as well have stayed home!* she thought. When Miguel said he was going to lead the mule to the stream, Josefina jumped up.

"May I go, too?" she asked eagerly. Anything was better than stirring stew and roasting herself by the fire like a *chile!*

"Sí . . ." Carmen began to say.

But in her eagerness Josefina had spoken too loudly and awakened Antonio. The baby began fussing and crying so much that he woke Juan, too.

Carmen rocked Antonio in her arms, but his wails only grew louder. "Antonio is hungry," she said. "I'll have to take him to Ana so that she can nurse him."

Carmen looked at Josefina. "You must stay here and look after Juan. And keep an eye on the lunch."

"I will," sighed Josefina, sinking down next to the fire again.

As soon as Miguel and Carmen left, Juan spoke up. "I want lunch now," he said. "I'm hungry."

Josefina couldn't help grinning. "You're always hungry," she said. "We can't have lunch until everyone comes back from picking nuts."

"I want to pick nuts, too!" said Juan.

"We don't have a sack," Josefina answered.

Juan pointed to the sack the lunch was packed in. "I want *this* sack," he said. He started to untie it.

Josefina could see that she had better find something for Juan to do, or he'd never stop pestering her. Maybe they *could* use the lunch sack. She and Juan wouldn't go far. She could keep an eye on the lunch while they gathered nuts.

Josefina covered the fire with ashes and moved the stew away from the heat. Then she helped Juan untie the lunch sack and empty it. She folded a corner of the blanket over the lunch. "Come on," she said. "We'll pick up the nuts that have fallen from the trees around here."

Juan happily took her hand. "We'll find the most nuts of anyone," he said, "and get the reward!"

Josefina looked at Juan's big brown eyes so full of hope. She didn't have the heart to tell him that they'd surely collect the *fewest* nuts of anyone. "We'll do our best," she said.

She and Juan did try hard. Juan scurried from tree to tree and pounced on every nut, crying, "Here's one!" But there weren't very many piñón trees near the clearing. Even after they'd gathered every single nut under every single tree, their sack was still pitifully light.

"This isn't enough!" Juan said, holding up the nearly empty bag. "We need more."

Josefina felt sorry for him. "I have an idea!" she said. "I'll shake the trunks of the trees to make the nuts fall down. I've seen Papá do it." Josefina wrapped her arms around the trunk of the nearest piñón tree and shook it as hard as she could. But only a few handfuls of nuts fell. Juan collected them and dropped them into the bag. They made no difference at all.

Juan sighed. "The tree is too big," he said, "and you are too small."

"Sí," agreed Josefina. Juan was right. Her skinny arms and legs were more the size of the branches of the tree than the sturdy trunk. She gazed up into the branches waving gracefully above her head, and all at once she had another idea.

"I'll climb up and bounce on the branches," she said to Juan. "That'll make the nuts fall!"

Josefina clambered up the tree. For the first time that day, she was *glad* she was so small. None of her sisters would have fitted between the prickly, pokey, needly branches of the tree as she did.

Josefina stood on a branch, held on to the trunk of the tree, bent her knees, and bounced. The branch dipped and swayed under her weight, and the piñón nuts fell like rain all around Juan.

Juan crowed with delight as he collected the nuts. "Do it again, Josefina!" he cried. "Bounce some more!"

Josefina did. And after she had bounced on every possible branch on *that* tree, she and Juan moved on to another tree, and another, and another, each tree a little bit farther away from the clearing. With every bounce on every branch, nuts showered down, pelting Juan and plopping to the ground. Juan cheerfully put them in his sack, which grew fatter and fatter.

Josefina was scratched and her hair was full of twigs, but she didn't care. As she bounced on the highest branch of the tallest piñón tree of all, she looked back toward the clearing. Something moving near the campfire caught her eye.

Oh no! There was a squirrel, bold as could be, nibbling at the lunch! "Shoo! Shoo! Shoo!" Josefina shouted at the squirrel as she frantically scrambled down the tree. "Quick, Juan! Run back! There's a squirrel eating the lunch!"

Juan hurried, but his fat little legs couldn't carry him very fast. The squirrel wasn't the least bit afraid. With its tiny front paws it took something that was

small and brown from the lunch and
popped it into its mouth before
it skittered away. By the time
Josefina was on the ground, the
squirrel was up a tall cottonwood tree.
Josefina saw the tip of its feathery tail
disappearing into a hole in the tree's
trunk.

Juan and Josefina stood at the
bottom of the tree staring up. "You bad
squirrel!" yelled Juan. "You stealer! Come
back!"

As if it understood, the squirrel came
out of its hole. This time it had a piñón
nut in its paws.

"Where did you get that nut?"
Josefina asked the squirrel. "Not from

our lunch. And your hole is not in a piñón tree."

The squirrel looked at Josefina with its bright, mischievous eyes. Then it scampered farther up the tree and balanced on a branch, chattering and scolding.

Suddenly, Josefina felt excited. "That squirrel is trying to distract us," she said, "and I bet I know why. Quick, Juan! Get the sack."

The cottonwood tree did not have low branches, so Josefina had to hug the trunk and shinny up to the branch just below the squirrel's hole. She reached into the hole and then whooped for joy. "Juan!" she shouted. "The hole is full of nuts! Hundreds and hundreds of nuts!"

"Hurray!" shouted Juan. Josefina tossed down handful after handful of nuts. Juan stood below, holding out his arms and smiling as nuts fell all around him. *Plip, plop, plippetty, ploppetty, plip!*

"Josefina!" exclaimed Tía Dolores. "You and Juan have done a lovely job of setting out the lunch for us. Gracias."

Josefina beamed. She and Juan had spread the lunch out on the blanket, so that it was ready and waiting when everyone returned to the clearing. There was soft, white goat cheese, ripe plums, small sweet apples, spicy chile stew, and

Josefina tossed down handful after handful of nuts.

cold meat. There were *tortillas* and big, round *buñuelos* in the bread basket.

tortillas and buñuelos

Francisca sank to her knees on the blanket and sighed dramatically. "I'm sure I collected the most nuts," she said. "My sack's so heavy it made me tired to carry it."

"Mine's heavier!" said Clara.

"No, it isn't," said Francisca.

"Yes, it is!" said Clara.

Papá held up his hand to stop them. "Let's see, shall we?" he said.

Francisca, Clara, Ana, Tía Dolores, and Papá put their sacks all in a line. "Well," said Papá after he had lifted each one. "All the sacks are quite heavy.

You've all done a fine job, but I think the heaviest sack belongs to—"

"Excuse me, Papá," Josefina interrupted. "Juan and I collected nuts, too. We'd like to ask you to lift our sack."

Josefina heard Francisca whisper to Clara, "Poor Josefina! There's not a way in the world she and Juan could have collected as many nuts as either one of *us!*"

"Where is your sack?" asked Papá.

Juan and Josefina grinned at each other. "There it is!" cried Juan, pointing. "Under the big tree!"

Everyone looked and gasped. The sack was bulging! It was much fatter than any of the other sacks. Juan and Josefina's sack was filled to the top, almost *overflowing* with nuts!

Papá laughed out loud. He walked over to the tree, grasped the sack in two hands, and pretended to struggle to lift it. "Bless my soul!" he said. "This sack is the heaviest by far. It's easy to see who collected the most nuts this year!" He smiled at Josefina and Juan. "Well done, little ones," he said. "You deserve the reward." Papá came back to the blanket and looked through the lunch. Then he looked again, and again. At last he said, "I'm sorry, children. I can't find the reward. It was a *piloncillo*, a little cone of hard brown sugar. I wonder what happened to it."

Juan and Josefina grinned at each other again. "A squirrel stole it!" said Juan.

"That's too bad!" said Papá.

"Sí," said Josefina. "But it's only fair. You see, Juan and I stole the squirrel's piñón nuts. I climbed up the tree and found them in his hole."

"María Josefina Montoya!" exclaimed Tía Dolores. "I thought you were an extraordinary girl the first moment I met you, and now I'm sure of it! How clever of you—and you, too, Juan." Tía Dolores hugged Juan, and then she hugged Josefina. As she did, she whispered in Josefina's ear, "I am proud of you."

Josefina hugged Tía Dolores back.

She was *glad* the squirrel had stolen
the reward of brown sugar. For her, no
reward on earth could be sweeter than
Tía Dolores's praise.

LOOKING BACK

HARVEST TIME IN 1824

The Montoyas gathered piñón nuts during the autumn harvest, but there was work to do on the rancho all year round. Men and boys worked in the fields and tended animals, and girls and women cooked, gardened, and tended the home. Families built their ranchos near rivers and streams. In the dry land of New

The rancho provided everything the family needed to survive.

Mexico, water was their most important resource.

Streams brought melting snow from the mountains to the dry land. Farmers planted their crops near a stream and dug networks of *acequias*, or irrigation ditches, to carry water from the stream to their crops.

Several families shared one main acequia. A *mayordomo*, or elected official, was in charge of it. He decided how much water each rancho was allowed

The main acequia in Albuquerque in the 1880s

and when the rancho was scheduled to receive water.

In the spring, the acequias had to be

cleaned. All of the families who lived on the acequia worked together to clear it of mud, grass, and stones.

Each family cleared the acequias that flowed into their own fields.

By late spring, the acequias were clean and overflowing with water. Now the growing season could begin.

Farmers planted crops that were originally from Spain, such as wheat, carrots, and apricots. They also planted native foods like squash, beans, and corn.

Each spring, the women and children gave their homes and churches a fresh coat of *adobe*, or mud plaster. Children loved to spread the plaster on the walls with their bare hands and smooth the plaster on the roof with their bare feet!

Girls and women also planted kitchen gardens in the spring. They grew fresh vegetables, fruits, and herbs that they used every day.

Girls plastering the walls of their rancho

Through the summer, families tended and watered their gardens and crops. The women and girls carried water in large pottery jars, called *tinajas*, from the stream to the gardens. The families had to make sure they had healthy, plentiful crops so the food would last through the winter.

tinaja

When fall came, it was time to harvest the gardens and fields. The men brought in the crops from the fields. The girls and women gathered crops from the gardens and orchards and preserved food for the winter.

Drying corn and chiles

Corn was an important harvest crop. Girls and women ground dried kernels into flour for tortillas. They also roasted ears of corn in an *horno*. Roasted corn was eaten as a sweet snack, called *chicos*, or soaked in lime and boiled for a stew called *posole*.

*This woman is roasting corn in an **horno**, or outdoor oven.*

The girls and women also preserved fruits, vegetables, and herbs from the kitchen garden. They strung chile *ristras* and slices of squash to dry, they buried melons in sand to keep them fresh, and they hung herbs to dry in bunches near the kitchen hearth.

Meat was also preserved in the fall. Animals from the family's herds of goats, sheep, and cattle were butchered. Then the meat was cut into thin strips and dried in the open air.

*Meat was dried in thin strips, called **jerky**.*

While the people worked, they had fun sharing gossip and news, telling stories, and singing songs. The harvest was hard work, but it was important to make sure everyone had enough food for the winter. If a family had a bad harvest, neighbors made sure they didn't go hungry.

Toward the end of the harvest, it was time to gather piñón nuts. Piñón trees provided wood for fires and nuts for food. Piñón nuts were also a valuable trade item. A good crop of piñón nuts came only every few years, so it was cause for celebration. The fastest way to gather the nuts that were still on the tree was to shake the tree until the nuts fell like rain! Once all the nuts were gathered, families could look forward to winter evenings roasting and eating the sweet nuts before the fire.

Piñón nuts were ripe when the cones fell from the trees.

AGAIN,
JOSEFINA!

Josefina slid her hand along the piano's smooth surface and admired the way the firelight was reflected in the shiny, polished wood. It was a cold evening, and Josefina and her family were gathered around the hearth in the family *sala*. Josefina was supposed to be knitting, but she couldn't resist touching the piano. It was so beautiful! Her aunt, Tía Dolores, had brought it all the way from

Mexico City when she'd come to live with Josefina's family on their *rancho*.

Tía Dolores glanced up now and smiled at Josefina. "You love the piano, don't you, Josefina?" she said.

"*Sí*," said Josefina earnestly. "I do."

Papá put down the piece of harness he was mending and asked politely, "Please, Dolores, won't you play for us?"

"Oh, yes, please play!" said Josefina and her sisters Ana, Francisca, and Clara.

"Very well," said Tía Dolores. She sat at the piano and began to play a soft, sweet song. Josefina thought it sounded like a lullaby that a mother might sing to her baby. She couldn't help swaying back and forth in time to the music. Papá and all her sisters had dreamy, faraway looks on their faces, as if they were remembering something happy. The music seemed to have cast a spell over them.

As Josefina watched Tía Dolores's hands gracefully moving over the keys, she was filled with longing. Oh, how she wished she could make music, too!

When the song ended, Josefina burst out, "Tía Dolores, do you think I could learn to play? Would you teach me?"

Tía Dolores looked pleased. "You must ask your papá," she said. "If he gives his permission, then I'll be glad to teach you."

Josefina turned to Papá. "May I, Papá?" she asked.

"May I, Papá?" Josefina asked.

Papá thought for a moment and then answered slowly. "You have many responsibilities, Josefina," he said. "Your sister Ana depends on you to help her look after her littlest boy, Antonio. And all of us depend on you to do your chores. Can you meet your responsibilities and take piano lessons, too?"

"Sí, Papá!" said Josefina.

But Papá still did not say yes. "It's not easy to learn to play the piano," he said. "It takes time and practice and patience. And even then, not everyone has a gift the way your Tía Dolores does. Are you ready to work very hard? Because if you aren't serious, you'll waste Tía Dolores's time."

"I'll try my best," said Josefina.
"I promise."

"All right, then," said Papá, smiling
at her eagerness. He turned to Tía Dolores.
"This is very kind of you," he said.

"Oh, it will be a pleasure!" said
Tía Dolores. "I've already seen what a
good student Josefina is while
I've been teaching the girls
to read and write."

"Sí," said Ana, the eldest
sister. "Josefina's the quickest of us all.
She's the best student."

Josefina bent her head to hide her
pleased smile. She knew that what Ana
said was true, and it made her quite
proud.

"You're all good students," said Tía Dolores to the sisters. "Would any of you like to learn to play the piano, too?"

"No, thank you," said Ana sweetly. "I wouldn't like to be the center of attention the way you are when you play the piano. It would make me nervous to have so many people looking at me."

"Oh, that wouldn't bother *me!*" said Francisca. "But I don't want to learn to play, because if I'm sitting on the piano bench playing music at a party, then I can't be dancing! Where's the fun in that?"

Everyone laughed except Clara, who shook her head at Francisca's silliness. Then Clara said,

"Frankly, I don't see the purpose of learning to play the piano. Making music just isn't practical. It's not like weaving, where you have cloth to show for all your work."

"Well," said Tía Dolores, smiling at Josefina. "I guess you are my only piano student. We'll begin tomorrow morning."

Josefina smiled back. "I can't wait!" she said. She felt excited and eager and confident. Soon, *soon*, she'd be able to play enchanting music just as Tía Dolores did!

✳

"Again, Josefina," said Tía Dolores.

"Sí," said Josefina. She tried hard not to sigh as she struggled for what seemed like the hundredth time to play the notes correctly. Were *all* her piano lessons going to be as long and discouraging as this first one? Learning to play the piano was not at all what Josefina had expected. It was much harder. There was so much to remember! And Tía Dolores was so strict!

"Keep your feet flat on the floor," Tía Dolores had said at the beginning of the lesson. "Keep your back straight. Keep your shoulders square. Keep your wrists level with your arms. Keep your fingers curved, as if you were holding a ball."

By now, Josefina ached all over. She slumped a little bit, and Tía Dolores tapped her back. "Up straight, Josefina," she said. "Now, try it again. Begin with the thumb of your right hand and play the notes up—*one, two, three, four, five.* And then down—*five, four, three, two, one.* Then switch to your left hand. Begin with your thumb and play the notes down—*five, four, three, two, one.* And then up—*one, two, three, four, five.*"

Josefina tried, but somehow her fingers would not do what she wanted them to do, and her left thumb hit the wrong note. Instantly, Tía Dolores said, "Start over. Remember, fingers curved. Back straight. Now, again, Josefina."

I wouldn't mind being uncomfortable, thought Josefina, *if only I were making music.* But so far, all she'd played was the same ten notes over and over again. It didn't sound like music. It sounded like water dripping into a puddle! It was not the least bit pretty. *Especially since I never do it without making a mistake,* thought

145

Josefina nervously. And of course the more she worried about making mistakes, the more she made. She was sure Tía Dolores must think she was terrible!

But when the lesson finally came to an end, Tía Dolores seemed cheerful enough. "Practice between lessons," she said. "That's the way to improve."

"Sí, Tía Dolores," said Josefina. She thought, *I certainly can't get any worse!*

That very afternoon, when it was time for her to take care of Ana's little boy, Antonio, Josefina put him in his cradle. Antonio looked surprised, because Josefina usually played with him. "I want you to sleep now," Josefina said firmly, "so I can go practice the piano."

Josefina rocked Antonio gently and sang to him. His eyelids drooped, then closed.

Good! thought Josefina.

But the second she stopped singing, Antonio's big brown eyes popped open, and he was wide awake. "More!" he demanded.

Josefina groaned. "You're not going to fall asleep, are you?" she asked Antonio.

Antonio just smiled and reached his arms to her. "Up!" he said.

Josefina lifted him out of his cradle. She could see that Antonio was not going to let her play the piano when she was supposed to be playing with *him.*

Over the next few weeks, it never got any easier to find time to practice between lessons. Lessons didn't get any easier, either. Josefina began to dread them. It seemed to her that Tía Dolores winced whenever she hit a sour note, which was often. She was sure that Tía Dolores must be tired of saying, "Again, Josefina. Try it again."

One day, Josefina hurried through her afternoon chores so that she'd have a few minutes to practice before it was time to help prepare dinner. She sat at

the piano and dutifully practiced the
tiresome, tuneless exercises Tía Dolores
was trying to teach her. She hit lots of
wrong notes, as usual.

Suddenly Josefina was aware of
giggling behind her. She looked over
her shoulder, and there was Francisca,
pretending to dance to her playing.
Francisca swooped around the room,
then tripped over her own feet. She
looked as clumsy as Josefina's music
sounded. Clara was watching, trying
to stifle her giggles.

Josefina stopped playing.

"Oh, don't stop!" teased Francisca.
"I want to finish my dance."

"Sí," added Clara. "Play it again."

Usually Josefina could laugh when her sisters teased her. But right now all her frustration and disenchantment with the piano boiled over. "Stop it!" she said sharply.

"Oh, Josefina, don't be so cross," said Francisca. "We were just having fun with your music."

"The music is not fun for *me*," said Josefina grimly. "I make too many mistakes."

Clara and Francisca exchanged a glance.

"Papá warned you, Josefina," said Clara matter-of-factly. "But you wouldn't listen. You probably thought that learning to play the piano would

come as easily to you as reading and writing did." She shook her head. "Well, I think you'd better face the fact that it does not."

Josefina could not stand to hear another word—even though she knew Clara was right. With a tremendous *bang!* she slammed the lid shut over the keys.

She grabbed her shawl, ran out of the room, and did not stop running until she reached the stream.

Josefina sank down on the rocky bank and sat hidden under her shawl with her arms wrapped around her knees and her head bowed. She felt angry at the piano, angry at her sisters, angry at Tía Dolores, and, most of all, angry at herself for being such a failure.

"Josefina, child, what's the matter?" someone asked.

It was Papá.

Josefina jumped to her feet to stand politely in front of her father. "Please, Papá," she said. "I want to stop taking piano lessons."

Papá frowned. "Tía Dolores has been generous enough to spend time teaching you," he said. "It would be disrespectful of you to quit now. Why do you want to?"

Josefina answered in a small voice. "Because I'm doing so badly."

"In that case," said Papá firmly, "you'll just have to practice more."

More? Josefina's heart sank. Practicing already used up every free minute she had, and she couldn't neglect her chores! "I just don't know where I'll find the time," she said.

Papá raised his eyebrows. "Look harder," he said.

Josefina could think of only one thing to do, and that was to do two things at once. She decided she'd have to start practicing at the same time that she was doing her chores.

She began the very next day.

Josefina pretended to be sitting up straight on the piano bench when she was really sitting on a stool husking corn. She pretended the kitchen table was the keyboard, and she played imaginary notes with the fingers of one hand while she was stirring a bowl of chiles with the other hand. She practiced curving her fingers properly while she was taking apples

154

one by one out of the storage bin, and she kept her wrists level with her arms while she carded wool. When she went to the stream to get water for the household, she hummed the notes from her lessons over and over until they were fixed in her brain.

After a few days, her fingers worked a *little* better at lessons. Tía Dolores rewarded her by giving her a song to learn. It was only a short song with a simple tune, but it sounded very pretty when Tía Dolores played it. Josefina was pleased. At last she'd be making music! But when Josefina tried to play the song, her fingers stumbled so badly that the tune was lost in wrong notes.

One afternoon, after her lesson with Tía Dolores, Josefina had a few extra minutes before she had to take care of Antonio. She sat by herself at the piano and tried to play the simple tune Tía Dolores was teaching her. She didn't realize that anyone had come into the room until Ana tapped her on the shoulder.

"I'm sorry to interrupt your practice," said Ana. "But I need you to look after Antonio." Antonio squirmed out of Ana's arms to get to the floor. Then he began in his funny, staggering way to walk to Josefina.

Josefina held her arms out to Antonio. "I'm glad to stop playing," she said to Ana. "I'm only making mistakes anyway."

Ana smiled sympathetically.

Josefina scooped up Antonio and hugged him. She smiled a cheerless smile at Ana. "I know I'm terrible," she said. "It's embarrassing! I'd like to give up." She admitted the truth to Ana. "If I can't play well, I don't want to play at all."

"Oh," said Ana. "I hope you won't give up. I've been watching, and I've seen how you've been trying to practice while you're doing chores." She nodded at Antonio, who was busy tugging on Josefina's braid. "I don't know if my

157

fine fellow here will let you practice or not. But give it a try." Then Ana kissed Antonio's cheek and left.

Josefina held Antonio on her lap and looked him in the eye. "Watch out," she warned him. "I'm going to practice. It'll sound so bad it'll probably make you cry!"

Antonio gave Josefina a happy, drooly, baby grin as she gently put him on the floor. He stood next to the piano bench and slapped the top with his hand, as if he were saying, "Begin!"

When Josefina began to play, Antonio crowed with delight. He bounced himself up and down on his chubby legs in time to the music. He bounced with

Antonio bounced himself up and down on his chubby legs in time to the music.

so much enthusiasm that he fell, *plop*, on his bottom.

Josefina stopped playing to help him, but he popped back up to his feet by himself and said, "Again, Josefina! Again!"

Josefina laughed out loud. "At least *someone* likes my music!" she said. Josefina was so cheered, she played the song again. She stopped worrying about making mistakes and played just for the fun of it. Pretty soon, Antonio began to dance. He'd take a few steps and fall, then get right back up, spin around, and fall again. But he never cried, and he never gave up. He kept trying to dance, even though he was really terrible at it.

He was giggling so hard he couldn't even *walk* three steps without falling.

As she watched Antonio, Josefina realized, *No one expects Antonio to walk perfectly. He's just learning. And no one expects me to play the piano perfectly, either, because I'm just learning, too.*

Josefina felt happier at the piano than she ever had before. She played her song louder and faster, again and again. She was making lots of mistakes. But Antonio didn't care, and neither did she!

Josefina was surprised when she heard someone clapping behind her. She stopped playing and turned to see Papá. He was smiling.

"Well!" said Papá. "That didn't

sound as if it were being played by someone who wanted to give up music."

Josefina smiled back at Papá. "I don't want to give it up anymore," she said.

"That's good!" said Papá. He bent down to pick up Antonio, who was pulling on his pants leg. "What made you change your mind?"

Josefina laughed. "Antonio did," she said. "I played a song that Tía Dolores taught me, and he really liked it."

"May I hear your song?" asked Papá.

"Sí!" answered Josefina with a big grin. "I'm happy to play it again."

LOOKING BACK

RANCHO LIFE
IN 1824

A New Mexican landscape

Life was hard for New Mexican settlers like the Montoyas. It was difficult to raise crops and animals on the dry, mountainous land. Drought was a constant worry, and so were sudden floods. Lightning, mountain lions, and rattlesnakes killed farm animals, and sometimes even people. Music brought a welcome break from all the work and worry.

There was no television or radio on the New Mexican frontier, and even books were rare. Settlers counted on musicians for laughter and entertainment. Music often provided a reason for the people of a village to gather together and

A musician playing his guitar

laugh and share stories. Music was a part of every celebration.

Settlers had many occasions to celebrate. The return of a trading caravan, the arrival of family or friends from another village, and weddings and baptisms were all cause for a *fandango*, or informal dance. On the day of a fandango, musicians rode a wagon through the countryside to announce the fandango. Some people would join the group, following along to wherever the fandango was to be held. By evening, everyone knew where to gather for the party.

A woman dressed for a fandango

As soon as darkness fell, the dancing would begin. To start the fun, the first

Musicians announcing a fandango

dance might be the *vals de la escoba,* or "dance of the broom." The guests lined up on both sides of the room. One boy would begin dancing with a broom. When he dropped the broom, that was the signal for everyone to find a partner as fast as possible!

Another popular dance was the *vals chiquiao,* or "courting dance." When

A courting couple dancing

a couple are courting, they are getting to know each other. During this waltz, the musician picked out couples to play a game. The girl was seated in a chair. Her partner had to kneel before her and make up a verse of poetry. If she didn't like his verse, she wouldn't finish the dance with him! The verses were often silly, such as:

Milk I like
And coffee too.
But more I like
To dance with you!

Music and song weren't just for celebrations. They brightened the settlers' daily chores, too. There was even a song about sweeping:

I sing while I sweep my room,
'Tis then I delight in song.
All women while they're sweeping
Sing as they wield the broom.
Forgotten are sadness and weeping,
And boredom takes his flight!

Broom

Parents also used music to teach children Spanish history and pass along their traditions, faith, and values. Many

New Mexican settlers had no opportunity to learn to read and write. Their wisdom was passed on to their children through stories, sayings, poems, and songs they knew by heart. Some songs had religious themes, and others told of Spanish kings and queens and the history of Spain. Parents also shared entertaining stories, called *cuentos*, or sayings, called *dichos*, that taught a lesson. Tía Dolores often

A Spanish king and queen

repeated the dicho "The saints cry over lost time" to remind Josefina and her sisters to keep busy.

Musicians and singers usually had

no formal music train-
ing. They played simple
handmade guitars and
violins. A piano like Tía
Dolores's was rare on the New
Mexican frontier! But musicians
were highly honored by the people.
Many made their living traveling
from village to village. They sang
ballads, or long stories set to music, in
exchange for food and lodging.

Learning to play an instrument
like the guitar or piano was certainly
difficult, as Josefina found out, but being
able to bring happiness to the people
around her made all the hard work
worthwhile.

JOSEFINA'S SONG

JOSEFINA'S
SONG

Josefina kicked off her moccasins and
waded into the stream. The water
swirled around her legs. It felt silky and
cold. She scooped up some to drink, then
patted her cheeks with her wet hands.

"I wish I were one of Papá's sheep,"
she said to her sisters, who were washing
clothes. "Then I'd spend the summer in
the mountains, where it's cool."

Ana and Clara laughed. But Francisca
bleated like a sheep. "Baa!" she said.

"Who cares about the mountains? *I* want to go to Santa Fe next month when the wagon train arrives."

"Me, too!" agreed all the sisters. The wagon train was coming from the United States. The sisters were eager to see the wonderful things like tools, books, buttons, shoes, and beautiful material for dresses that the *americanos* would bring to sell or trade.

"We shouldn't get our hopes up," said Clara, wringing water out of a sock. "Papá hasn't said that he'll take us with him. He has business to do."

The sisters knew Clara was right. Papá was going to Santa Fe to trade mules for sheep. There'd been a terrible flood in the fall, and many sheep were drowned. Papá needed to build up his flock again. Sheep provided meat for eating and wool for weaving and trading. The *rancho* couldn't survive without them.

"I'm sure Papá will take us," Josefina said cheerfully. "And he'll trade his mules for hundreds of sheep. It will be just like in the shepherds' song." She sang:

> *Happy shepherds,*
> *goodness has triumphed!*
> *Heaven has opened!*
> *Life has been born.*

When she finished, Josefina was surprised to see that Papá had come to the stream. "You sing that song beautifully, child," he said.

"*Gracias,* Papá," said Josefina, blushing at his praise. "The shepherd Santiago taught it to me."

"Ah, yes," said Papá. "Santiago and his grandson Angelito are your friends, aren't they?"

"*Sí,*" said Josefina, "though I see them only in the winter." During the warm months, Santiago and Angelito lived up in the mountains, tending part of Papá's flock. "Santiago loves living on the mountain. He said that he and Angelito would rather be there than anywhere else on earth. But I do miss them."

"Well," said Papá, "I'm going to visit them tomorrow. I heard that Santiago was ill. I want to be sure he's better.

Would you like to come, too?"

"Oh, sí, Papá!" said Josefina with all her heart.

"Good," said Papá. "We'll leave early in the morning."

He turned to go, but Francisca stepped forward. "Pardon me, Papá," she said. "Since you are speaking of traveling, I thought I might ask, have you decided if my sisters and I may go to Santa Fe with you next month?"

"I haven't decided," Papá said. "I'll see how well Josefina does on our trip up the mountain tomorrow."

The second Papá was gone, Francisca spun around and demanded, "Josefina, did you hear what Papá said?"

179

Francisca spun around and demanded, "Josefina, did you hear what Papá said?"

"Yes!" said Josefina joyfully. "I'm going to see my friends! I'll sing with Santiago. Angelito and I—"

"Not *that!*" Francisca cut in. "I meant what Papá said about watching you. Your trip tomorrow will be a test. You must behave perfectly. Don't be any trouble. Don't slow Papá down. Don't complain about being tired or hungry or thirsty."

"I won't," said Josefina. "I'll sing all the way."

"No! Don't!" said Clara. "Be quiet! Don't annoy Papá or you'll ruin our chances of going to Santa Fe."

"And if you do," said Francisca, "we'll never speak to you again!"

"Don't worry," said Josefina, grinning.

"I'll be perfect. After all, I want to go to Santa Fe as much as you do."

It was easy for Josefina to follow Francisca's advice. Even after she and Papá had been riding for hours, Josefina was too delighted by all she was seeing to be tired or hungry or thirsty. But it was *not* easy to be quiet. Josefina wanted to sing along with the wind, chirp back to the birds, and ask Papá hundreds of questions. But she remembered Clara's advice and never made a sound.

"You're so quiet," Papá said as they stopped to let the horses drink from the stream.

"I'd expected my little bird to be singing all morning. Is the ride too hard for you?"

"No, Papá!" Josefina exclaimed quickly.

"Good," said Papá. "Anyway, it's not much longer now."

In a few minutes, Papá and Josefina heard the clear, high sound of Santiago's flute. As they rode into the little clearing, Josefina saw Santiago sitting by the fire outside his tent. He had a lamb in his lap.

"*Buenos días,* Santiago," Papá called out. "God be with you."

"Is that you, *patrón*?" said Santiago, standing up.

"Sí, and my daughter Josefina," said Papá as they got off their horses.

"*Señorita* Josefina!" said Santiago.

"Welcome!"

"Gracias, Santiago," said Josefina, smiling at her friend. But her smile faded when she looked more closely at Santiago's face. His eyes were flat and lifeless. Josefina gasped and quickly looked at Papá. She could tell by his unhappy expression that he'd realized it, too. Santiago was blind! Josefina felt her own eyes fill with tears.

Santiago bowed. "Your visit honors me," he said.

"It is our pleasure," said Papá kindly. He went to Santiago and put his hand on the old man's shoulder. "How are you?" he asked.

"By God's grace, my illness is over,"

said Santiago. "I'm as strong as ever. But my sight is gone. I am blind."

"I'm sorry," said Papá. Josefina saw a look of deep concern on his face. Then he asked, "Where is Angelito?"

"He's with the sheep," said Santiago. "He watches the flock now while I tend our camp." Santiago picked up the lamb that had been in his lap. "I care for the sheep that are hurt, or sick, or orphaned like this fellow."

"A shepherd's life is not easy. There's much to do," said Papá, patting the lamb. He turned to Josefina. "Go tell Angelito I wish to see him."

"Sí, Papá," said Josefina. She hurried up the steep path that led to the pasture.

It felt wonderful to stretch her legs after the long ride.

She was out of breath by the time she saw Angelito. He was near the stream, watching the sheep grazing on its banks. The stream was narrow here, just a swift ribbon of water that slid between the rocks.

"Angelito!" Josefina called.

Angelito looked up and waved. He whistled to the dogs, signaling them to circle the sheep and keep them from wandering. Only when the dogs were in place did he hurry toward Josefina, covering the distance in a few graceful leaps. Angelito was nine years old and small for his age, but he was fast. As he came near, Josefina

saw that his face didn't look as merry as usual.

"Señorita Josefina," Angelito asked, "why are you here?" Then he remembered his manners. "Pardon me," he said. "I meant, buenos días. I hope that you and your family are well."

"By the grace of God, we are," said

Josefina. "My papá has come to see your grandfather." Josefina paused, then said, "Oh, Angelito! How long has Santiago been blind?"

Angelito sighed. "Early this summer my grandfather was sick with a fever," he explained. "After the fever went away, he couldn't see at all." Angelito looked earnestly at Josefina. "But he doesn't need to see!" he said. "I can see for him! I watch the sheep now. The dogs obey me. I know this mountain better than anyone. I know all the sheep in our flock, too. I won't let any of them get lost." He patted the slingshot tucked in his belt. "When bears or wolves come

around, I scare them away." Angelito
hesitated, then asked, "Your papá hasn't
. . . he hasn't come to take our flock
away from my grandfather and me, has
he? My grandfather would die if he had
to leave here. The mountains are home
to him. And to me, too."

"My father knows that," said Josefina.
"He would never ask you to leave." But
a tiny, terrible doubt crept into her mind,
and her voice was worried as she said,
"At least, I don't believe he would." She
beckoned to Angelito. "Come, now. He
wants to see you."

Angelito and Josefina went down the
path back to the tent. Santiago was stirring
a spicy-smelling *atolé* stew over the fire

and cooking *tortillas.* Josefina was amazed by how handy he was. Though he could not see, he never faltered or dropped anything as he cooked and served the food. After the meal, Santiago played his flute. The old man's fingers moved quickly, never hitting a wrong note. Angelito's voice blended with the flute in lovely harmony as he sang the *corrido*—a song that he and Santiago had made up about their pleasant, peaceful life on the mountain caring for the sheep and sleeping under the stars.

After the song, Angelito rose to go back to the flock.

"Stay, Angelito," said Papá. He turned to Santiago. "Your song reminds

me of the days when I was a boy and
you worked for my father and sang your
corridos for him," he said. "You've been
a faithful servant to my family for many
years. I thank you for your loyalty and
hard work."

"Bless you, patrón," said Santiago.

"Amigo," said Papá, "I worry for your
safety. I'm afraid your blindness makes it
dangerous for you to live here, so far from
other people. I'm afraid it's dangerous for
the sheep, too. A blind shepherd can't keep
watch over a flock, and the sheep are too
valuable to be entrusted to a child as young
as Angelito." Papá's voice was gentle. "I
think the time has come for you to rest,"
he said. "You and Angelito can come live

on the rancho. I'll send another shepherd
up here to take over your duties."

Oh, no! thought Josefina. "Don't, Papá!"
she burst out passionately. "You mustn't!"

Papá frowned. "My child," he said
gravely. "Be still."

"Papá, I'm sorry. But I must speak,"
said Josefina. "Santiago and Angelito can
care for the flock if they do it together.
Angelito is Santiago's eyes. He's a fine
shepherd. He's brave and fast and careful!
He'll keep the sheep safe, and Santiago will
keep them well." Josefina knew she was
doing exactly what her sisters had warned
her not to do. She was making Papá angry.
But she couldn't help it! "Please, Papá,"
she pleaded. "Don't take their flock away.

You mustn't make them leave the mountain. It's their *home*."

Papá stood. Josefina had seldom seen him look so stern. In a solemn voice he said to Santiago, "I beg you to excuse my daughter's disrespect. I see now that it was a mistake to bring her." Without looking at Josefina, he said, "Wait by the horses."

Josefina did as she was told. When Papá came, she climbed back up on her horse and waved a sad good-bye to her two friends. *What have I done?* she thought as she rode away. *Nothing good. I didn't change Papá's mind. Santiago and Angelito are still going to lose their flock. All I did was make Papá ashamed of me, and so angry that I've surely ruined any chance of going to*

Santa Fe. My sisters will be furious with me!

Josefina, lost in her own dark sorrow, didn't notice that the sky was darkening, too, though it was only midday. After she and Papá had ridden for an hour or so, Josefina felt cold. She shivered, and looked at the sky. A huge black cloud loomed from behind the mountain and blocked the sun. The wind began to blow hard, and then, all in a rush, the rain came. It lashed at Josefina so fiercely that she could hardly see. She pulled her *rebozo* over her head and huddled close to her horse's neck, keeping her eyes fixed on Papá as he rode in front of her. Overhead, the trees swayed crazily in the wind. Underfoot, the path was soon slippery from the rain.

Thunder rumbled in the distance, and then—*crrrack!* A bolt of lightning ripped the sky. With a terrified squeal, Papá's horse reared up. Its hooves pawed the air wildly. To her horror, Josefina saw Papá fall off his horse and land hard on the rocky ground.

"Papá!" she shrieked. His horse whinnied, then bolted off down the mountain, dragging its reins behind it. Quickly Josefina slid off her horse. "Papá, are you all right?" she asked, kneeling next to him.

"My . . . leg," Papá panted. He tried to sit up, then sank back again, his eyes squeezed shut in pain.

God help me! prayed Josefina, shaking from cold and fear. She knew she had to get Papá to shelter, but where? Home was too far away. Josefina made her voice sound steady. "Papá," she said, "if I help you onto my horse, do you think you can ride back to Santiago's camp?"

Papá nodded. It took all Josefina's strength to help Papá struggle to his feet and mount her horse. When he was settled, she took the reins and started to walk back up the mountain. Again and again she slipped on the rocky path. Again and again her horse stumbled.

The wind raged and the rain fell harder than ever, but Josefina kept on. The stream that had been a thin trickle earlier in the day rushed by now, churning brown and angry.

Then at last, over the noise of the storm and the stream, Josefina heard a shout. She looked up and saw Angelito running toward her.

"My father is hurt!" Josefina called out. "Please, he needs help."

Angelito didn't say a word. He took off his *sarape* and wrapped it around Josefina. Then he took the horse's reins and led the way to the tent.

Josefina crawled inside while Santiago helped Papá off the horse. The sides of the

The wind raged and the rain fell harder than ever,
but Josefina kept on.

tent flapped and billowed in the wind, but inside it was dry and cozy. Santiago made Papá comfortable on a bed of sheepskins. Gently, he felt along the bone of Papá's leg.

"A bad sprain," he said. "It's not broken, thank God." Josefina watched as Santiago rubbed ointment on Papá's leg and then carefully, tenderly, made a splint of a blanket and some strips of leather. "This will hold your leg straight," Santiago said. "It will be as good as new in a few weeks. But you must lie still now, patrón. Rest."

"Gracias, amigo," said Papá. Then he asked, "Where is Angelito?"

"He's taking Josefina's horse to a safe place," said Santiago. "Then he'll keep watch over the sheep to be sure no harm comes to them. He said that he'll stay with them until the storm is over."

Papá nodded. He reached for Josefina's hand, then closed his eyes. But he was restless. Josefina could tell that his leg pained him too much to let him sleep.

"You and I must take his mind off his pain," said Santiago. He took out his flute. "Sing with me," he said, smiling at Josefina.

So Josefina sang. For hours, she sang along with Santiago's flute. She sang all the songs she knew, and then she sang them again. When she ran out of songs, she began to make one up herself. It was

a *corrido* about her trip up the mountain with Papá. She sang about her eagerness to see Santiago and Angelito, about her outspokenness and Papá's anger, about the storm, Papá's accident, and, at last, Santiago's comfort and care. She sang about Angelito's bravery in staying with the sheep through the rainy night.

Josefina's throat was tired. Her eyelids drooped and she ached with sleepiness, but she didn't stop singing. And deep into the night, Santiago played his flute for her and for Papá.

❄

When at last the long night was over, several men from the rancho appeared. Papá's horse had returned to the stable, so they'd known right away that something was wrong and had headed up the mountain to find Papá and Josefina.

"We are in good hands, as you can see," Papá said to them.

Santiago built a fire and made hot tea for everyone. Then

Angelito brought Josefina's horse, and the men helped Papá and Josefina mount up and prepare to go back down the mountain.

Before they left, Papá leaned down from his horse to shake Santiago's hand. "Old friend," he said, "thank you for your help."

"It was my honor," said Santiago.

Papá straightened. "You cared for me so well," he said. "I know that if any of my sheep were hurt, you'd care for them well, too." He turned to Angelito. "And you, my boy, were as brave and hardworking last night as any man three times your age." Papá's voice was serious. "I spoke hastily when I said that it was time for you two to come live on the rancho. I hope you will stay here. I'd be proud to leave my sheep in your care."

Josefina's heart rose. She smiled at Angelito, and he smiled back happily. Santiago bowed and said, "Gracias, patrón. We'll stay."

Josefina waved good-bye as she and Papá set off. After they'd gone a short way, Papá said, "You must be tired, Josefina."

"Oh, no, Papá," said Josefina, even though she was.

"You were very brave yesterday," said Papá. "And I know that you didn't sleep all night. I heard you singing to me. I especially liked the corrido you made up about our adventure on the

mountain." He grinned. "Perhaps when
we go to Santa Fe with your sisters,
you'll sing that song again."

Josefina laughed aloud with joy and
relief. Papá had forgiven her! Tired as she
was, she said eagerly, "Sí, Papá, I'll sing
it then. I'll sing it now, too." And she did,
all the way home.

LOOKING BACK

SHEEP IN 1824

The rancho provided almost everything that families like Josefina's needed
to live. The sheep on the rancho were
especially valued for
their meat and
wool, used to
make warm
clothing.

Churro sheep

In the
1500s, the
Spanish
brought the
first sheep to
New Mexico.

These small, sturdy sheep called *churros*
were used to the dry, mountainous land.
Their wool was long and thick, which

*Sheepskins were used for
the lining of a baby's cradle.*

made it good for spinning and dyeing.

Families like the Montoyas owned
a few hundred sheep. For most of the
year, the family's sheep were kept on
the rancho. *Pastores*, or shepherds, like
Santiago watched over them.
In the summer, when the
lower lands became hot
and dry, the shepherds
took the sheep into the
cool mountains.

The shepherds set
up camp near a pasture

*Many churros had horns
pointing in all directions!*

and a river or stream. Each morning they herded the sheep to fresh grass. When the sun went down, they herded the sheep back to camp. In the evenings, the shepherds played music on their flutes and told stories. Sometimes they carved animals out of wood.

Often dogs were the only company a shepherd had. The dogs were always on the alert for coyotes, wolves, and bears, and they also helped keep the sheep together. When a sheep strayed too far from the flock, the dog would guide it back, sometimes even nipping the sheep as a warning. At night, the dogs' sheepskin beds were spread out in a protective circle around the flock.

The dogs also protected the sheep if the camp was attacked by Comanche, Apache, or Navajo Indians. These people were *nomadic*, which means

An Apache warrior in 1828

they moved their homes seasonally. Nomadic Indians and New Mexican settlers were enemies. They raided each other's homes, stole animals, and took people captive. If raiders were spotted, shepherds sent the dogs to scatter the flock. But the shepherds knew this would not save all of the sheep—some of them would be stolen.

Guns and ammunition were scarce on the frontier, so a slingshot and stone was usually a shepherd's only weapon. But most shepherds had good aim—they had lots of time to practice shooting at rocks or trees while the sheep grazed.

The shepherds also protected the sheep from bad weather. In the mountains, lightning and floods came on suddenly. They could harm or even kill many sheep in an instant. The shepherds had to act quickly to move the sheep to a safer spot, such as a cave, a woods, or higher ground.

At the end of the summer, the shepherds herded the sheep down from

A flash flood in New Mexico

the mountains to the pastures near the rancho. As winter neared, the sheep were moved closer and closer to the rancho.

In the spring, when the sheep's wool was the thickest, it was time to *shear* the sheep, or shave off their wool. Men used metal shears to cut the sheep's fleeces, one by one. A skilled shearer could cut off a fleece in one piece.

Once the thick coats had been sheared, the sheep were ready for the hot summer. The shepherds moved the sheep back up to the mountains to start the cycle all over again!

Abuelita *(ah-bweh-LEE-tah)*—Grandma

Abuelito *(ah-bweh-LEE-toh)*—Grandpa

acequia *(ah-SEH-kee-ah)*—a ditch made to carry water to a farmer's fields

adobe *(ah-DOH-beh)*—a building material made of earth mixed with straw and water

americanos *(ah-meh-ree-KAH-nohs)*—men from the United States

amigo *(ah-MEE-go)*—friend

atolé *(ah-TOH-leh)*—corn mush or porridge

banco *(BAHN-koh)*—a low bench built into the wall

buenos días *(BWEH-nohs DEE-ahs)*—good morning

buñuelo *(boo-nyoo-EH-lo)*—fried bread served with a glaze or with sugar and cinnamon

cañaigre *(kah-NYAH-gray)*—a flowering plant that grows in the Southwest. Cañaigre roots are used to make gold, orange, and brown dyes.

capulín *(kah-poo-LEEN)*—also known as chokecherry. Berries were used for dyes as well as jam, jelly, and stomach medicine.

chicos *(CHEE-kohs)*—corn on the cob that has been roasted, steamed, and dried

churros *(CHOO-rohs)*—small, sturdy sheep

corrido *(koh-REE-doh)*—a song

cuentos *(KWEN-tohs)*—stories or folktales

dichos *(DEE-chohs)*—proverbs or wise sayings

empanadita *(em-pah-nah-DEE-tah)*—a small pie or tart filled with fruit, nuts, or meat

fandango *(fahn-DAHN-go)*—a big celebration or party that includes a lively dance

gracias *(GRAH-see-ahs)*—thank you

gran sala *(grahn SAH-lah)*—the biggest room in the house, used for special events and formal occasions

horno *(OR-no)*—an outdoor oven made of adobe

la vaquerita *(lah vah-keh-REE-tah)*—the little cowgirl

mantón *(mahn-TOHN)*—an embroidered silk shawl

mayordomo *(mah-yor-DOH-mo)*—a man who is elected to take charge of the acequia

padre *(PAH-dreh)*—the title for a priest. It means "Father."

pastel *(pah-STEL)*—a pastry filled with fruit

pastores *(pahs-TOH-rehs)*—shepherds

patrón *(pah-TROHN)*—a man who has earned respect because he owns land and manages it well, and who is a good leader of his family and his workers

piloncillo *(pee-lohn-SEE-yo)*—a small sugar cone

piñón *(pee-NYOHN)*—a kind of short, scrubby pine that produces delicious nuts

posole *(po-SO-leh)*—a stew made of preserved corn

rancho *(RAHN-cho)*—a farm or ranch where crops are grown and animals are raised

rebozo *(reh-BO-so)*—a long shawl worn by girls and women

ristra *(REE-strah)*—a string of chiles

sala *(SAH-lah)*—a room in a house

Santa Fe *(SAHN-tah FEH)*—the capital city of New Mexico. Its name means "Holy Faith."

sarape *(sah-RAH-peh)*—a warm blanket that is wrapped around the shoulders or worn as a poncho

señorita *(seh-nyo-REE-tah)*—Miss or young lady

sí *(SEE)*—yes

tía *(TEE-ah)*—aunt

tinaja *(tee-NAH-hah)*—a large pottery jar used to carry water

tortilla *(tor-TEE-yah)*—a kind of flat, round bread made of corn or wheat

vals chiquiao *(vahls chee-kee-AH-o)*—courting dance

vals de la escoba *(vahls deh lah es-KO-bah)*—dance of
      the broom

VALERIE TRIPP

At 9   Now

Valerie Tripp says that she became a
writer because of the kind of person
she is. She says she's curious, and writing
requires you to be interested in everything.
Talking is her favorite sport, and writing is a
way of talking on paper. She's a daydreamer,
which helps her come up with her ideas.
And she loves words. She even loves the
struggle to come up with just the right words
as she writes and rewrites. Ms. Tripp lives in
Maryland with her husband and daughter.

JEAN-PAUL TIBBLES

Jean-Paul Tibbles lives in England with his wife, two daughters, and three cats. He enjoyed visiting Santa Fe and getting a feeling for Josefina's world.